1

Mitch Bensel

Shirley!
Thank You, for
Guessing!!
Enjoy my Rambling

Twitter Poetry ~ Love and Life

@Mitchrambling

Mitch Bensel

To all the amazing people I have interacted with on Twitter… thank you for the inspiration — and the RT's and tags!

"An enchanted moment"

Old Tree

I am an old tree
my branches know when the storms will destroy
when the sun will heal
rain's moisture flexes my strength
rest under me, my shade is real
my bark is jagged from age but strong
roots deep with experience
of the ways of time
lean against me
I have you

Scribbles

I am the scribbles that drop out of your mind
the pencil that has broken lead ...
the image that is scanned but for a moment
in your heart....
I am   ... drops of lost rain into memories
the bit of me ... seen
is not the depth of me ...
feel my music
I am

Mitch Bensel

False

overflowing passion onto the table of non
the grains of wood capture pieces of me
pushing into their want and take...
but is not love
is not love
another reaches for the drops staining the table
yes... my passion drips into them also
seeking the heat
that matches my soul\

Forever

I saw you walking along the beach
you smiled then slowed and turned
to me ... you spoke words of hello and
come this way
your legs carried heaven across the sands
lifting my vision against your lean
I felt eternity smash like a wave
moving us against and again
and repeat...

Vanish

spilled onto the ground of pleasure
drops of moisture grasp my mind
heart beats fast with the roll of her kiss
...I am afraid to exhale...
she may vanish

The Air

I became the air today mixed with rain
slowly covering her ache
... I was the piercing emotion of passion
pushing into her universe....
...I was the tornado of want
lifting ...her up.... against my storm
.... she came to me with a smile...
I was the kiss

Ecstasy

with a glance the first layer falls away
touch delves deeper
kiss to bring sweetest aroma
devouring
skin... heated
moans escape
defying gravity
soul becomes the dance
of two
of layers ...
secretly giving way
ecstasy

Lazy

Let's be lazy and scribble poems of dreams ... with wishes as the pen...

Heat of a Moment

within the heat of a moment
her kiss slipped beyond waves of forever
circled her desire with fingers of slow
encased self with rain
falling from her embrace
oh god never let this moment slow
... lifting into forever I slammed
into hope ... rested in her ocean

She

she is truth
love
beauty
life in one breath
sensuous
her kiss
just the touch of her lips....
causes ecstasy   ... heals all wounds
the world is a better place
because of
... she

Mitch Bensel

Your Kiss

I dreamed and yet awakened
with your kiss   mixed with mine
never has the day moved
in such a way…

Angel

put your kiss upon my soul
let it rest a spell
do not let it go … with that whisper of your
pure
put your hold upon my heart
ease it against tomorrow
dreams are made of these

Winds of Love

distant winds flying to find
my kiss   your touch
our breath   entwined
when they find   they lift to take
the two   of life forever true
you see they belong not of this place
they have to return
becoming the
breeze floating away

Lines

I am the lines on a sheet of paper
pushed into life with black lead
moved along slicing the brains eye
with thoughts
dribbled deeper
the pencil lifts
end of my life
waiting   on a sheet of paper
for your press against my soul

You

I am hungry for your words
your voice needs to ease into me
your skin needs me to lightly touch
leaning against   ... we need to kiss
oh my my   what you do to me

Sliced

sliced into time
between tomorrow's wishes
yesterday's pain
the battle constant
it aches with heated anger
defeat is its reward
ripping apart soul of light
its need
within escape is your angel
easily repelling
the hunger of the demon

Time

I held hands with time
... came in the form of rain
it slipped easily into my hold
falling from forever ago
... I think I know I think I ... felt
... love with a hint of always

With Me

I want to know you
thoughts worries dreams
hold my hand
walk in the sunrise
dream with me
laugh with me
let me inhale you
souls will know
such joy
passion
love

Dream Me

dream me a memory tonight

spill me with water from tears

of ...that place they call joy

follow my whisper today

carry it with you into your smile

hold the pain for a moment

... for

me

Forever

fell asleep on a whisper

was the air or her … kiss

or the touch of her smile

rolled over onto a dream

moved inside to feel the sun's heat

… stood next to forever

she took my hand   . . .

walked into the sunset

ignited by it's heat

forever please....

us

Beauty of a Woman

for the feel of a woman
the softness of velvet... her passion
does hide ... the taste
of a woman her skin beyond   time ...
can move a mountain
and a heart to become blind
with a beat and a rush
she can hold eternity with her
eyes
leaving man lost   in the waves ...
of surprise

Yum

lie with me on this night
capture my sigh as it
escapes into the softness
of your
touch ...

Us

Moaning into the nights air
my flesh on fire
feeling our heat move like
waves across the room
arching   yearning
needing to fill
we moan
shifting with time
slowly
move with me

Billion Pieces

I wonder …
can a soul rupture into a billion pieces of love
surrounding theirs
turning into stars …
ever shining …
also I am over tired
I miss her
need tomorrow to get here
the end

Universe of Love

... sometimes this poet has no words
for words do not find the heat of her passion in my soul
so I will just wait and let her heart whisper in my dreams
while my soul becomes a universe of love

Desire

feel me explore
shhhh
I know ...
lift
ecstasy

Mitch Bensel

Wuss

sometimes I can't like the wuss in me
... strong but weak with her hello
I mean... c'mon
grow some
nah
like light that cannot help but shine
her hello captures me
a footstool I would be
a blanket
the water in her shower
the mirror on her wall
sigh

Touched by an Angel

I have been touched by purity of light

she is an angel of heart

of soul

of flesh

and she ... let me

fall into

her

... if today took me away

my soul would be complete

Feed Me

maybe taste more than wine in my soul tonight

… sip some pleasure of a memory

but is it a memory if it is the wallpaper of my soul

part of my heart's beat is hers …

cool against my desire

sipping on a memory

refreshing … devouring

my ache

Cotton Dreams

something about cotton ... not sure what
maybe youth and times of no air conditioning
... cotton t-shirts
sweat from playing hard outside
the smell of her kiss on my cheek
her cotton dress blew in the wind
... cotton and women
they seem to go way back in my life

Into The Night

close to me
I pull you
we move into the night
let's dance upon these rain drops
and shift within this light ...
of ... softness that surrounds
and lush ...lips that whisper
move a little closer
let me taste your delight
of our lift our sway   our us
into the night

Scattered

where she is concerned I am
... insatiable ...

Mitch Bensel

Write about the Sunset

I tried to write about the sunset ...
but the heat of you against me ...
became the glow.
I wanted to tell of the cool waters near
but   the way of us between time's kiss
moistened my lips
I tried to tell of the tree that swayed with the breeze
felt you dance with me

Wisps of Love

i watch as you lift
you move like the softest breeze
feet flow ... across
like a stream
of freshest water ... refreshing
beautiful
arms float with wisps of love

Mitch Bensel

Waves of Pleasure

i watch as you turn
swaying curves entice me
waves of pleasure slowly
caress me
the light has become you
glowing against the air
i watch....my breath move to yours
carried by your smile
gently pulled
i whisper and inhale
your kiss...

Soul's Touch

when you feel the air swing by you
tugging at your cotton t-shirt
and feel her hand tracing your arm
then it settles into your hand...
the flash of her on your bed…
skin alive with heat
want... desire ... my soul ...
lost in hers and ... I like it there

Thoughts

I can't think of ...
wait I want to feel more of ...
the wind told me today that the sun held my secret love ...
I flexed my wings and jumped into the breeze ...
melt me with your heat ...
life is nothing without you near ...
said my mind to a thought

Calming thoughts

closing my eyes to see
a way of light to thee
before the next second comes to life
your heart will feel
and slow beats will whisper
your soul ... will calm
... closing your eyes to see
always with you
is me

Mitch Bensel

Mantra

cannot keep my hands off
of her ... hello
cannot whisper enough
into her soul
will not stop
making love ...
laughing with her
settles dust of old pain
into a far away drain
insatiable is my new mantra
she is my voice

Mine

falling asleep with her in my arms
what is better in life
nothing   not cotton candy
or the best bourbon
her heat waits for me to open
her soul pulls me inside with a glance
this is what they write of in books ...
... and she ...
is
mine

Her Whisper

I was strong against the winds of their wants
...I gave with all that was to be me
false was the truth
... so I freed myself from that marriage
tree
through the many women I wandered
into and beyond and lifted
none of them entered my soul
like her whisper slips into me

Silken Dream

I leaned into a wish
it had a silken chord with a pillow near
I rested my head on the pillow
my breath released ...
easy was the moment she came to me
whispering   ...."you are mine"

Forever I Hope

my mind's eye saw
my women of past hello
my flesh remembered their touch
shallow truth be told...
contrast to now
she can kiss me just right
beyond my skin it moves
into my heart's soul   so bright
I will dance with this way of lift
and play   forever I hope

Smile

her beauty comes from the depth of her being
she doesn't just 'smile'
she exudes love ... and it trips over itself to
fall into me
she doesn't just kiss me ...
passion's heat pours into me
as we breathe each other in ...
she ... is my soul's light

Mitch Bensel

Let's

let's make love in the ocean
let's fall asleep on the beach
hold my hand and tell me your dreams
... whisper your passion to me
kiss my heart with that wonderful smile
that you carry in your soul   ...

Mine

you are mine
he whispered as she kissed his soul
I will take what I want
he said ...with low tone
she leaned back
allowing
... I am yours
the mix was complete
the bond was made
... forever had a new dream

Swimming in Love

vast is the ocean of her heart
have you gone swimming in love
covered with peace wrapped in
arousal …

Never To End

falling asleep with her mouth close
… feeling her breath on my neck ...
her leg over me   her warmth against
how can I sleep   kissing her softly she awakens
more than her mind
the pleasure begins   hoping never to end

Mitch Bensel

To Me

there is a storm brewing in my soul
... is off to the right just a little
a little near my heart ...
as the winds move my ache
of love
is she near
or   far with her sails filling
to carry her finally
... to me

Pitch of my Soul

with every thought ... or action or mis-direction
slight variations of levels of distraction
playful boring ... slightly disturbing
sweetly whispering ...sometimes glistening
running with that swift way... slowing every day...
... only and only ...and only she...
knows my silent wish... my passion free
within that within... she knows
the pitch of my soul

Mitch Bensel

Silence of Her

silence ...
she can find no words she
lifts against my slow of glance
she sighs ... and then i know
my trance has been
broken
into
silence of her

Ache

heat ... oh it is nothing
compared to my ache for you
now
desire ... I laugh at its folly
of being a feeling of ooo la la
love ... ah there it is
the word that matches now
need to soon
lift into that horizon
where passion only dreams to fly
slammed shut it did
opening it slowly back to light
why dost this happen
go thither doubt
come hither true
... I hate this hue

Mitch Bensel

Interesting

interesting moment when an inhale becomes ecstasy of her kiss ...
exhale becomes a reach for more

I Saw You

I saw you
the sun said hello
… you opened your arms leaned back
your hair became a million sparkles
I sat on the beach ... watching
the ocean whispered
you leaned forward
your skin became a million fireflies
lifting you into the air
... I saw you

Lightning

lightning is the rip
of someone's soul as another leaves them
thunder is the rage of pain as the tear
digs its claws into the fabric of your essence
...
mayhaps this is why we like to make love
during thunderstorms #rebirth

Gone

it's ok if you want to say goodbye ...
I was never there
it's ok if you say thank you for your love
... it has already left
it's ok if you rip my soul
and throw it to another's grip
have the t-shirt
... so
I guess
everything is ok
lessons in life in love are not easy
it's ok if you say ...

Rested

my soul lay bare against the cool breeze
... your essence
I felt ... surrounded by your beauty of
time ... of smile of ease
I rested

Twinkle in Your Eyes

with a smile that never hides...
if you love simply but deeply
c'mere, we have to talk
let's walk through the rains that hold the air
drink its touch against our fears
pull the heat of sunlight across our skin
resting within
…kiss...

Mitch Bensel

Let's Art

...the background is my way of hello
the colors are your whispers into my dreams
let's make some art
let others feel our passion

close to me

we move into the night
let's dance upon these rain drops
and shift within this light..

Mitch Bensel

Let Me Know

of   softness that surrounds
and lush   lips that whisper
move a little closer
let me taste ...let me know

Hello

the blue days of night
those ones of cool
memories of hot
thoughts of ... gone
new day has a few pebbles of hope
... scrambling between my words
I whisper...
hello

Mitch Bensel

Run With Love

maybe, could it be
that love just isn't near my cup o tea
alone methinks into tomorrow
and past the wink of her sexy hello
... but hey I love the way of time and sun
laughter is easy to cause the soul
to run with love and life and tease and a wink
poets can be strange :)

Skin Deep

all of these images tossed about
naked this and that
within is the truth
I have been with the beauties of
skin ... the beautiful of oo la la
beneath was ... nothing
no individuality.
my point to say ... my wish to make
the old adage beauty is only skin deep
runs true   with many

Sleep

I watched you sleep
the air caressed you   hovered
across
my mouth followed the air
fingers slow onto ... against
lips follow the lines of trace
pressing ... tongue becomes
touch...
lowering myself you hold me
guide me... yes...
open for me

No Bother

I wonder when
my mind left
my common sense
my trust of way
it could have been
it may be so
I thought you were
what you said
but hey is cool and to be true
have a good day
won't bother
you

Kiss

is easy to use words
to tell of how and how
to make love to a woman.
... time and
time and many   come to mind
within their passion
is your map to define
listen with your kiss
she will never lie

Get Ready

tender

like

belly exposed

... is my soul

kind of threw the walls to the floor

aching ...wishing

wanting

the taste ...

the passion the   moans

the lift

I miss

will wait for the right   walk

time and place

but darlin

get ready

Us

I have seen

... you have also

and we are still ... making it work

Desired Taste

is it just me or
after she has her run
her sweat falling across and down
to taste her sweat
pressing against the heated skin
through clothes now wet
Is it just me or
oh yes

Women

falling out of the blue of a wave
that one of altered dimensions and
dammit   those sways
of her hips... her walk
or just her smile
.... women ...will be the death of me
but what.
a
way
to
die

Her Move

she moved through the sunlight
I had hidden in my heart
... each step allowed
her kiss fell to my desires
she was   against me
owned me
I am usually the one
that takes
I let her do what she wanted
she moved through my
passion with kisses
of delight

Your Kiss

I dreamed and yet awakened
with your kiss   mixed with mine
never has the day moved
in such a way…

A Wish

One day ...
every moment will be to love ...
make love
.... walk with ...
make love ...
to you

Mitch Bensel

Her Waves

once ...
i fell into her waves ...
she lifted me
i fell again
i lifted her
thrown into the universe we
like a light that escapes behind an exhale
became

Whispered This Morning

I whispered this morning
was a quiet easy whisper
was a wish   of a thought
that escaped a moment
of a time   that slid off the clock
into my whisper
to you

Waiting

I am an easy soul
weathered the hurricanes
of their desires
survived to walk the beach alone
agates are magic
jaspers are cool
my heart still waits
for your whisper to soothe

Beauty in Tears

walking in your sleep
your feet never touch the ground
... being in her soul
your ache never dies down
... life is a tease
with her wish to please
... when you wake
be ready
to cry

When I Knew

I knew when you walked away

...

the last night we made love

lingering was the kiss

slow was the release

we ... outgrew

each of different grains

of sand...

I knew I would always

love you...

I always   and still do

... when I knew

Onto Her

when the moment ...
is
every way of touch should begin
from mouth   fingers   to skin
on   and on without slow
she should feel you explore
every piece of glistening
warm
sigh   just let her know you want all of her
... fell out of the poem
into her

Mitch Bensel

Emotion of a Wish

enter the emotion of a wish
to wish
the wash of ache that depth
of desire that way of   want
other ways I cannot say or find
words do not compare nor twist
levitation desired
across and through
your passion my exhale
a wish

Soul's Room

took time to the side
asked it a question
what should I wear when I meet her?
time smiled
your soul
falling inside myself I picked up the room
dusted off the pieces
waited for her hello
shined with new to create new paths
across her skin into her heart

I Saw the Sunrise

Looking through the oceans walk
I saw the sunrise ...
your smile and my
... ease into forever

Heaven's Moment

there is a moment in time
when you pull her close
bodies as one
the beach is near
and the sun is hot
but that moment ... with her against
her lips near
is heaven

Lost In You

today is new with flavor
dots know the rhyme
my pencil cannot write
without your whisper into
... have to ponder this

C'mon Over

enjoyed the soft of love
and have known
the hard of hatred
each moments of dark
or light the in between grays and
the walk of my way given
my soul   a new coat of paint
the white to get whiter
the light to shine through
now I wish
to walk   those miles
with you.

Mitch Bensel

She Smiled

shhhh she whispered
my legs were weak
... c'mere   she beckoned
my breath was slowed
kiss me ... she winked
my body alive
passion divides
the ...way of kiss of time and
us...
now   she smiled

She Walked Into My Arms

she walked into my arms
was a breeze within my soul
she smiled ...
her body pressed against me
... my soul flew
seeking her depth
finding her wish
she walked into my heart

Mitch Bensel

False Again

the taste left
after the sheets of easy
tore your flesh
no feel   just feel
slipped inside her heat
scorched my heart
... the taste
left ... dripping down
to the floor
of regret

Wind

have you ever felt the wind...
seduce your soul
oh yes
moans escaping
while your body swayed
have you ever   dreamed a   kiss
that you felt   with the night
yet no lips pressed against   only the wind
so light

Mitch Bensel

Arts Lover

the paper becomes her soft lift under
my touch   my kiss
the paint is my passion desire
to fill her   with
if only art was as easy as making love
I would be ... a good ... well yea

Gone Love

when did it change
this feeling
did it rain
and I had my hood up
did the snow cover
with whitest calm
and my eyes were closed?

Mitch Bensel

Us

into our dance as we climb
our tree ...   so impossible
to see   without
rhythm   of her
without rhythm
of me...

Only Me

I am the only the one
the one...
she knows...
whose touch will never
burn into wings of flight

Heated Lust

kind of craving you right now
I mean   shall we dance
against the wall
beneath the stars...
let nature watch
our scent will arouse
the night will moan
I am here...
your swollen desires
found
my push of desire
allow and   open
satisfy my craving
… soon

Come Here

was walking through your mind last night
while lying upon my bed
sheets were cool
close to me
was your desire and easy kiss
I saw all of your pain
your love   your... ache
I loved this walk into and across
you
come to me   tonight
open the way for us
...kiss

Mitch Bensel

Secrets

secrets lie in the glance of a touch
whispers seduce with the slow of across
leaning to feel   wanting to hear
every moment of you ...
listening to...
my kiss ...my hands   my flesh
mouth to consume
your way of want   is my wish to give
... shhhh secrets

Waiting

the night holds my heart with memories
circling my ache with your scent
tipping the drink to my lips
I taste your kiss
is obvious I am inside the tornado
of your essence
... like a butterfly
waiting for a breeze
to carry me to you

Harmonica Dreams

I write words and attempt to play the harmonica
walk the beach in search of magical rocks
whisper to nothing in hopes I am heard
dream of love
walk with life
broken a bit am I
but know this
my soul pushes deeper than
any touch you have felt
caverns of love in my heart
seek to hold you

Lace

you wore the lace
my mouth removed   slowly
you wore the heels ...that dug
into my back
you wore me   into the night and day
you are still   in my heart
my soul   my kiss holds your smile
I am an island in your soul's ocean
wash this from me please
free me or hold me once more

Do You Ever

do you ever hear a song
and taste their kiss
walking ...feel them against
fleeting is the way of touch
the deepest push of time
always gets dressed and leaves
do you ever hear the love in your heart
softly wish for one
one to finish life with
to know their depth
do you ever . . .

Maybe

maybe my touch is the one
that will never escape your breath
maybe my kiss will encapsulate your love
with passion and desire
maybe I could just be the one to walk
beside and with ... in time through time
... inside a wish is a dream
inside a dream is ecstasy of
a smile
maybe...

Spice of Your Smile

I want to taste the spice in your smile
inhale the fragrance of your words
... walk with your dreams
lift into your clouds of emotions
....wash my soul with your kiss

Overwhelmed

she moved with me so wonderfully
her lips teased me with words
lightly touching my mouth
usually I am the one that causes the stir
her tongue traced   I allowed
waited
her hurricane of passion overwhelmed
me

Mitch Bensel

ecstasy

interesting moment when an inhale becomes ecstasy of her kiss....
exhale becomes a reach for more

Library

there is a library in my soul
of ... love and memories of flight
whenever I need... I just open
the memory of her...
we were like silk against satin
to the stars was easy lift
depth of ocean's magic
just an inhale
my library of us
in my soul

For Me

forever is a place of washed jeans
and shoes that are stripped of white
flung across the sands
dashed into the dots of wasted moments
lost upon those waves that the ocean
the waves
the beach
i find again my dreams across this beach for there she is
walking seeking   and aching for me

Forever Please

I don't want to love you ...
Just because you love me I don't want to kiss you
Just because you want a kiss
I want to be with someone to be with
through all of life
I don't want to be alive without you
find me

I Saw You

I saw you ...
the sun said hello
you opened your arms   leaned back
your hair became a million sparkles
I sat on the beach   watching
the ocean then whispered
you leaned forward
your skin became a million fireflies
lifting you into the air
... I saw you

Coffee Shop

she was sitting in the coffee shop
.... her hair just touched her shoulders...
slight movement ....she crossed her legs.
... wrapping the present

I spilled my coffee

Missed Her

I missed her
... like the wind needs to push through
I watched her
... as she ran toward me
into my arms she fell
her sweat against me
I wanted her
the bushes held the blankets
covering our fever
she was mine

Pondering

I was pondering a moment ago
about you
did ya feel me say hello.
my kiss was   soft
my wish was real
in this ponder ... I had a moment
ago...
dreams hold us at night
and you are in my dreams
slowly this heart
is saying   hello
in a ponder kind of way
while gathering my wits

Mitch Bensel

The Ex

picking up pieces of thrown darts from
the ex
I leaned and saw an angel
her passion is deep   her truth is
... true
what the hell am I going to do
... fly and see then taste maybe
... I am drugged by her presence

Passion

I wrote the book on passion
... I opened the valleys of desire
a kiss was found upon your lips
that was formed by my command
within the within is   forever
the light that thrusts   into softness
never leaves   never alone
shhhh   is my whisper ...
taste

thoughts

light pours gently
as my breath empties
onto her skin
she inhales my thoughts

Her Words

her words
I taste with sips of pleasure
feeling liquid heat
surround and fill
me

Mitch Bensel

Surely

surely
if I touch her soft velvet
with mere flesh
I will dissolve

Love Them Forever

when ... you find one
that allows you to be you...
when you…
find one that matches
your passion in ...a simple kiss
... when you
find one that always is there to hear
when you   find
let them be themselves …
let them have freedom ...
then pull them close
and love them forever

Mitch Bensel

Feel of a Woman

for the feel of a woman
the softness of velvet   her passion
does hide ... the taste
of a woman her skin beyond   time
can move a mountain
and a heart to become blind
with a beat and a rush
she can hold eternity with her
eyes
leaving man lost   in the waves
of surprise

Storm Brewing

there is a storm brewing in my soul
.... is off to the right just a little
a little near my heart ...
as the winds move my ache
of love ...
is she near
or   far with her sails filling
to carry her   finally
... to me

Mitch Bensel

Go Away

grasping the air
slamming against my chest
I pound your memory
from
me

Wash

wash off the night with her ...smile
stand through the push of
regret .... with her kiss
.... my mind seems to love to
want you near
I smile at this ...

Mitch Bensel

I could use

I could use a little of you today
smile as we sit
in silence ...
walk with me and dream
touch ... with gentle tease
...tease with more
then slow
... my soul is tired
tracing you with my wish
kiss me with that heat
of you   with me

not sure

ever whisper to the air and talk to

them… the one of your future...

you hope to spend

time   … love

heat   kisses   touch

oh my mind is lost now

in her openness for me

kiss and feel me darlin

soon

Mitch Bensel

See you ...

may have to give you up
may   need to walk with the air
of time and tomorrow
may have to rent a room in
your heart
to leave   or to go
may have to forget that thought
see you at noon

Sliced Thought

silenced with a thought of her
dropping imaginary scenes
with me   ...with she
I may be going crazy
this mind of mine
my wishes are beating up my dreams

Wrong Map

those walls we build
I   built
are damaged from our own love
for you see
it is so
... love breaks all doors
walls to flow back into your
soul
those walls ... just a veil
a reminder ... a lesson
of a glorious moment
time   a journey
just had the wrong
map

Dreaming of You

woke a bit early
dreams of scattered clothes
memories dropped sighs
laughter was new
drifting back to dream
finding you

Dance of Love

within the within of ... within
is a place waiting to be felt
floating in a liquid heat
yet calm ... sending smooth waves
easy lifts with slow drops
wonderful is the ache
to satisfy a hunger   will never happen here
for it is forever ...waiting
to begin again
the dance of love

Breathe

one more to say
my kiss on your skin
your soul
your heart
it sings a song of forever
pull the tab to accept me
into your
… breath

Mitch Bensel

Hello

whiskey just isn't smooth enough
wine drops me away into bubbles of nay
tequila does tease at first
the beverage that lifts … causes euphoria
me drinking her kiss ... lifting her against
liquid heat never slows
when you say hello.

Passion's Ache

I miss you
with every breath I exhale
I feel you
my hands trace you with pressure of want
skin hot ...breath fast
I look like a man that has a fever
I do
a fever to burn your kiss with passion's ache

Warmth of Her Touch

flesh consumed with desire
to be moistened by her lips
caressed by her breath
moving like light
dancing on the wind
I run
burning from the fire of her touch
overwhelmed with surges of pulsing passion
escape
before I never want to leave
the warmth of her touch

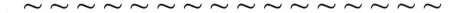

Mitch Bensel

~ Life ~

Something is Amiss

something is amiss
the light is beautiful the sun is bright
the breeze fills with hope and is cool against me
not looking forward to the
answer to this feel
may have to shut down the doors
and go home

Mitch Bensel

Past Haunts

swallowed into the crevices of the floor boards
between where dust lives and rats die
exhaled past
haunts me

P.S.

p.s. to life
step off of my doormat
wipe your feet somewhere else
back away from my window
screens keep out the bugs
my fan is on for my pleasure to feel
the air that holds no dust
I am so done with fake souls
that walk up my stairs
gone soon are these words

Mitch Bensel

Hope

droplets of hope fell upon my skin
splashing me with a spray of innocence
ripping from me all loss
i moved my hands
to cover myself with her light
consuming my soul
passion unmatched in my lifetime
i saw the star
as it first flew across
my life
she is mine

Escape

sitting at the bar the lights are low
they do that so you stay ya know
closed blinds and shaded lights
the ice in my bourbon made the familiar sound against
the crystal glass
my hand looked old
tipping the drink to my lips
to shade my soul
from pain's kiss
to escape but remain

In A Fog

cannot hear today
people talk but I am gone
I am in a fog of lost
not even beside   myself
or near myself
don't want to be near
myself
crushed is not good enough
... shattered is closer to the
thought if
I had a thought
writing is futile
but is what I do
I write

Sorrow

on the edge of sorrow
dripped against myself
the paint of me is disgust
the walk of me is non
why do I even breathe in the air
it will be hurt as it enters

Secrets

I found a whisper that was hidden

behind a thought

inside my heart

I never heard it

I closed

it is still there

Memories

I put my head down on the desk
to rest   to think
but school days of tv classes came to me
of sweet Rachel sitting next to me...
my head on my desk looking at her
dreaming of a kiss...
then getting hit on the head by my teacher

Mitch Bensel

Hope

skipped a rock across my soul today
it moved with good pace
the waves of my life gave many lifts
to the skip of way
... still watching it as I sit
near the ocean's push
into my heart.

Moments

like arranging an image
to capture a moment
put the flowers here next to the vase there
somehow … in that miracle way
you moved next to me
and now we
are the moment   … captured

Mitch Bensel

Word Party

imagine a word party
of poems and novels and non-fiction hellos
that fall across a bed at a hotel
the bourbon poured and the passion spilled
I would love to be part of that......
imagine

Poet

sometimes... just being near is enough
talking or silence
holding hands ...
I have become a poet in my moments
the drag of tongue across purpose of life
... sometimes
is more satisfying

Mitch Bensel

Shadows

shadows always near
more arrive as memories gather
their chatter is annoying

Addiction

Where do I put this pain …
waiting to hear you are gone ...
is late and time laughs at my soul ...
God take away her pain ...
hold her keep her safe
or take her home ...
your will be done

Mitch Bensel

A Good Day

I had a bad night last night
I let it cover me
with its pounding
of past and now
today I am tired from the battle
but today will be a good day …

Cycling

The last few miles
cycling this day
I thought why not
then the hills said ... nay
only with sweat and fatigue
will you climb our way
so there it was the few
rolling torturous lifts and drops
like an insatiable lover
the hills make you push
lift again   again again…

Mitch Bensel

Old Days

I miss the tie I wore
with crisp white shirt
the cuffs held
of memories at a dance
I miss the air of your smile
across my soul
the music the colors of your cheeks
flushed with desire
I miss the wooden floor
that soothed time
guiding us into a memory turned
to the wall
it ... knows all

Facade

drop away the image
that way you think I want
let your soul say hello
spill me your essence
the way of inner self
warm me
with your depth
the core of all
… drop away the image
tell me who you are
energy knows truth
and silly is the walk
of one that is not
... play not the game
I am beyond that rhyme

Mitch Bensel

Easy

I held hands with life
and got soaked ...
with easy smiles

Weathered Time

I am   weathered time
wind shifted layers of self
tested with all the sands blast
crooked with the tilt of spit
pushed with anger's laughter
elegant in strength
see the smooth of my worn walk
bring me your wish
will sift it through my soul
give it life

Mitch Bensel

Fluid Life

squinting through the day
many roads opened across a field
flowers fell away beside but stayed near
life   is fluid   moving forward
oh the joy to be had   laughter with love
to   hold deeply in our souls
opening my eyes wide I saw
life

Doors

What doors can be closed
those ones in your mind
which ones can be drugged shut
why can't it be quiet
the air is too loud
the light too bright
but the doors stay open

survive

wandering through my own halls
doors with pictures stuck to their
frames
I want to walk faster but move like
slow   slow liquid push I lean
repeating
a clock becomes lips that move
words slip across my chest
through my heart
my hand pushes the last door open
released

Time Ocean

I have crossed time
… like the ocean with waves
I have inhaled more than a tornado can lift
... I have been the way of their release
… now I ... watch to see ...wait
to know
if time is mocking me once more
or beckoning my truth

Mitch Bensel

Naps

when a nap comes to visit
... take it easily to your bed
ease against those sheets of cool
and warm your soul with rest
... awaken lost and not knowing where you are...
will remind you of youth
when you got drunk and woke up
in your front yard

Attire

words ... fall out of me and form incomplete sentences with proper
attire

Mitch Bensel

rain falls

the sound of the cleansing ...
the feel of its energy
thunder follows with a rip against time
easy on the soul
calming to my heart
sending love your way
with fresh rain to cove
rattling around in a cage
a rock that was found
dropped into a bucket of
common and gone
... waiting is my name
patience was my walk
afraid to touch the water
peace ... please find
hold her ... with your rhyme
said the poet to the dime

Rest

my eyes try to see
the light of this day
but all that happens is a blink
they are tired
do not look, they say to me with their
dryness and red
giving in to the sleepy of me
a nap will be my way to fall
into and beyond to dreams

Moment

follow the flow of this place

lift with ease ... know the kindness

love from real of depth

by truly . giving of self   our strength

our passion   our beauty

we build now

rest little ones .... this is only a moment

worry   little ones ....   this moment

creates your eternity

Forever

visited forever with my soul cleaned and waiting
to see if there was a star to drop
or a bit of light to finish my shine
of life of kiss of she I ...miss
a whisper with dots of sensual fell
down   across and into my shell
...to my soul it found me waiting
to hold with my kiss

Mitch Bensel

Youth

skipped a rock across the pond
it flew with dips and lifts
watched the water respond
with ripples walking to the edge
climbed the trees, saved the lady tied to the railroad tracks
...youth visits at times.

Survive

the dirt of the ground visits me at times
my face pushed into it
slammed by life
smashed into pain
but
I know how to roll over
and stand away
from   that moment
that hits me
from time to time

Rain Stopped

the rain stopped long ago
... ground soaked threshold
grasses tried to breathe
I walked under the trees
they wept ... absorbed their pain
they reached for me
to help
the burden of water released
saturated the ground even more
my feet soaked walked to the dry
the sidewalk ... away from

Secret Paths

rain finds secret paths...
eyes blind ... for the hands of ease
show the way tracing
yes the leaf green does fall
and the stream quick with life
does so flow   ....
but the rain   ... envelops
the soul

Mitch Bensel

Poets

poets know the dance
the lift
sometimes easy to read
other times you have to have a pass
to see the secrets

Forever's Hello

ever sip on a soda and watch
.... the sunset the lightning bugs
the way the trees go silent...
ever feel your heart
reach into forever for their hello
... crickets...

Out of Kilter

a little out of kilter
a bit off like …
an inch or a mm
… no rhythm, today is there
but swings in the wind
no one on the swing
just swinging
and
swinging
then a leaf falls and the ground
thunders me to my feet but where
and it is again the begin a little out of kilter

Anger

when will I learn to
let the rain contain my thoughts
dropping to find you
washed ashore between the rocks
whimpering and cold
alone   why again am I here
flirted with anger tasted its salt
rebound into the way of spit
I am where I belong
so be ... it

Mitch Bensel

The Rain

the rain may find its hold
and know the yellow of gold
across the dandelions breast ...
but the dandelion never hides
... always open ... always wise ...
soaking the rain within
dandelion dances ... through time

Words

eeny meeny miny mo
catch a word by its toe
if it hollers … let it know
you are the ink it's just
the flow

Mitch Bensel

Realities Time

drifting between realities
to feel your soul move through dimensions
… feel time like it is water
moving around driving between realities
cautiously

No Signal

... sitting in the living room
no signal walking across the tv screen ...
it is only partly on
but is on   repeating   repeating
no signal no signal ...
waiting to be complete
from another's energy

Mitch Bensel

Along a Path

I walked along a path
... the sun covered and lifted my spirit
I left behind ... yesterday
as I turned ... the path clean
with life, fresh, flowers ... sun

Soul

even the deepest
coldest loneliest
part of your soul
still has you with it... so   yea

Mitch Bensel

Convo

Hey … wanna go out and play … see a star   talk to the moon.

Dust

wrote upon a

that fell through the light

air slapped it across to the wall

floated to the way of gone

... to the other place

of tomorrow and forever

in between tomorrow you will find me

the one of easy to find

and easy to leave

the way of the fool

the way of non

I know its taste

I had her daily

every minute

she fed me with tease and no

away in the manger I will go

to rock in the chamber of

nevermore

Gathered

I was gathered up once
her smile became my breath
I was held against her wishes …
my body bent at her will
my explosions her toy
I was drained but ever was my
push …the thrust of self
into again   again
… her soul was the #Villain
of my recompense

Silence

silent inside

torn

again words did their thing

thrown at me

dicing the tendons of trust

with a spew from unknown thoughts

let me at least do the wrong

I am accused of ... just once

Against my Soul

ever it is and there it was
... a splat of anger mixed
against my soul
my love must cause another's soul to
relapse into past loves or ...
or ... I am to pack up my love
and keep it bundled deeply inside
self

Painting

about the way the pastel pushed against crisp white paper feels...
looks   comes to life with brilliance of colors images …

Mitch Bensel

Slipping

dipping my toes into the waters
fall against a splinter or two
heat holds
like it does
that liquid way of arousing
complete where only
slight moan or movement
entices the push
complete into the water
I ... slip ...

Light Dancing

is easier to sip from the cup of sorrow
than to dance with daylight
although and then … and always seems
light is magical
with it's calm smile
and lift

Mitch Bensel

Poem

I don't use big words
just simple deepest passion of thought
I don't don the clothes of better than
or the way of lift and slam
just sorrow from old love
gone and torn away
I don't plan on writing a poem
that would make   sense or feel
just a piece of myself
from that quilt

Tonight

tomorrow starts a new day

tonight

is always

tonight

Mitch Bensel

Between Lines

walked between lines of today
and tomorrow
...interesting was the flex of time
it laughed   then it slowed to
hello   ... for it had never been visited
in a rhyme
I tipped my hat and went on my way ...
a pleasant memory for this one of
words... between the lines

Universe of Beauty

once ...
i fell into her waves   she lifted me
i fell again   i lifted her
thrown into the universe
we
like a light that escapes
behind an exhale
or in a moment
time can turn into a beautiful flower
the sunlight's voice fills
our every inhale
in one moment ...
a universe of beauty can live

Goodbyes of Yesterday

I may be a bit broken
from the goodbye's of yesterday
but I am complete in self
my heart ... seeks the deepest level
then will tip toe through
inhaling your fragrance   seeing
the vast way of beauty
like flowers across a field
open for the sun   moving
with the breeze

Kinda Love

scattered in my thoughts
is your kiss
I remembered someone once
twice
well maybe more
that held me in the way of flow
and deep with a push to the side
... kind of love the way of me

Defeat to the Floor

dragons fly with fire
I fly with hope
tomorrow knows me already
... doors open
with that smile you cannot trust
but I have the way of know
and ... been there
with an easy flex
I bust the way defeat to the floor

......

Alone

'No man is an island entire of itself; every man
is a piece of the continent, a part of the main'
John Donne ...
Part... of an amazing poem by a poet of... life
but many are islands
with oceans
raping their beaches
raging against their loneliness
their loss
of self

Love Self

truly
if love cannot be of self
walls are impenetrable
to another's love
it will slide down
fall at the feet
of alone

"We Have You"

whispers were tangible
she walked into my soul
we dropped to the floor
I had her
... wide was her desire
deep was my want
liquid fire
cascaded down my flesh
explosion was fast
her smile turned into darkness
her skin withered away
she whispered
"we have you"

Mitch Bensel

Harmonica Writing

played the harmonica
then read some poetry
it's what I do
in case they don't like
poetry
but the harmonica was jealous
and captured my tongue
I couldn't read the words
only blow   and hum

Tequila Thoughts

my heart's broken
my soul is crooked
missing a sock
beside the tequila
sat the spider
her name was 'hello'

Mitch Bensel

Insomnia

sleep evades with a little smile
it knows you want it
teases you with moments of
comfortable
then speeds away   into the darkness
that you surround yourself with
pulling it along and away

Broken Soul

love breaks   the soul
with its touch
this body
becomes the slave to one
kiss
busted is this air
inside me for it searches only
for her hello
and lifts only
for her to breathe it inside
and hold forever
this broken soul

Lost Moment

missing a moment
had it   held it
it fell off my soul
somewhere between the toes
or down the hall of forever gone
dashed against regret
will never bring
a moment back

Mitchism

Don't get caught up in the tornadoes of other people's emotions

Mitch Bensel

Life

have seen the air move around
felt the rain coming down
falling across my skin of soul
never have i felt
a wish
beyond the touch of silken moisture
of earth's   dew of life
the soft of sheets cool to hold
me in the night

Sideways Man

call me the sideways man
to the side of
beside
always near but
never to smother
... sideways man
will never block your path
... always help with a wink
and a nod of ok
yea
call me the sideways man   always with ya
to the side ... winking as you walk
by

Mitch Bensel

Shadow

You can wear the shadow of yesterday ... like the clock on the wall ...

Find Self

if you can today
smile a wee bit and hug yourself
cuz hugs
and such wiggle your toes
walk in the sun
be the best you can
even when you are done
this is a rhyme with no design
to cram or make you cry
just a wish and a hope
with a dream to the side
for you to feel your soul

Mitch Bensel

Nothing Here

nothing is real
yet it slithers into you
they smile but
care nothing for you
the bounty is the wish
what can be had is
the dish
offer up nothing
walk away with a smile
you know the rhythm
and they
can't dance

Not Me

I was taken into a wave
the salt of the water was
bitter   the push into the sand
was painful
clarity became my friend
the fool was not me
in the end ...

My Boxers

me and my boxers　　... the perfect relationship
rainy days all good
sleep in... no problem
jogging... yea they don't know
universal they are with all emotions

My Walk

falling back inside the words
the shadow of their slant
rests easily with my walk
her kiss   their eyes
aching for more
settling for less
watch the clock do its thing
opening the worlds
whispering to
kissing   her
lifting more
pushing less
tasting all

Mitch Bensel

Reverberated

tried to speak
your voice smashed the air
the turbulence reverberated
against my mind
surrounded by yourself
must be a lonely place
I leave

Lack Of

inside the night
between a thought
doubt runs through
dangling its lack of's
into you

Hope

droplets of hope fell upon my skin

splashing me with its spray of innocence   lifting...

ripping from me all loss   pain

i saw the star

as it first flew across   my life

whispering

now it owns my kiss

Winds of March

thoughts of love
once crisp like the air
of autumn
now lost in the winds of
march

Mitch Bensel

My Silence

silence enters with shoes off
... brings a way of
easy   sometimes   shatters your core
memories like shreds of flesh
drop across your soul across your
heart. dropping you to your
floor of self
... waiting for the music of your hello
to comfort ... my silence

Music Saves

The shadows in a bar with music low ..
. carry a hint of tease where a mind may flow
... across the way she smiles ...
her drink is her love ....
the other one slows her tease and leans ...
candles know this heat ...
mixed with ...
incomplete ...
music saves my wandering mind ...

Digestion

Don't worry about the silence ...
you shoved the pain through my gut ...
digesting can be boring at times but
... this too shall pass

Soul Is Tired

a little tired this day
soul is sleepy or something
words fall from my being
tossed like popcorn through my veins
mayhaps   my soul needs a nap

...

Mitch Bensel

Life

I have known many women
I have tasted more than the salt
from tears that fell with cowardice ...
down and down
did you know
the levels of reality are not easy places
to live   they don't even like a fair
handshake

Out of Ink

I ran out of ink
from my soul to my blink
it was random   but the rays of light
fell across my page
giving me insight to the way of
sage
to feel and know that all is ok
but
I ran out of ink
smoke signals   ok?

Mitch Bensel

Memories

inside today is another
day
the pot of memories
where the air was of youth
passion was deep with
agony waiting to release

Whispered Pain

whispered once
felt the pain
... flew into the wall
with passion of heated flame
... thrashed in bed from agonies release
yelled at the stars
slept in the rain
... silenced the pain
whispered

Mitch Bensel

Poetic Pain

being poetic causes one to   remember
... pain never changes
its
clothes

Not My Style

I could write vaguely with imagery
stilled bricks with elusive
tongues   hidden in crevices
of her thoughts   his hands
their flesh
crimson flows
velvet holds
trepidation revealed
scantily clad among the damned
scalded into fires of
want

yea   not my style

Expectations

sitting back some
looking at life the way a
friend   looks at a friend
no expectations or walls
no need to hide because
friend
slip into the day
just being alive
you will see   so much
nothing has to be done
you don't have to shine
just be...
and ... breathe

Bears

might not be a good day to write stuff…
all grumpy inside myself...
beside myself...
and even over there to myself
spinning ...
without a motor
... will wear ya out
I know why bears hibernate
they just cant bare... the day

// groan//

Mitch Bensel

Dreams Broken

I woke up broken
left myself in a dream
of pleasure and peace

Today's Shadows

slam against life with its lack of
knock it back
stare at the words of filth it threw against
walk across the shadow

of past and now
today

Mitch Bensel

Wings

wings carry angels
time carries us …
laughter carries children
a frown knows the dust
walking is the work
the feet have to know
have to know   writing with toes
of smashed universes   in darkest shoes
laughing I have to smile at this sight

Drown

not much of much in this world
... poet ... writer lover
the ocean has my soul
neatly placed between every wave
... I drown every day
to be reborn with hope
that the next wave
will be her smile
her kiss
her   opening way
for me

Mitch Bensel

Light Seen

ever notice the light ...
from the side of tomorrow
when the windows seem afraid
and the night wants to
borrow just another   moment
from that   time
bricks
old   the key turned
the door opened
the steps held breath was young
breath is old
time is always so damned
cold

Goodbye

where are the words I need
where do they live
my lips have tried to kiss
them into reality
yet they dissolve

Mitch Bensel

Writer's Block

a word looked at me the other night
pulled up a chair
leaned some
"you think you a poet... you think you know"
I sat back
"I do all the work you throw me around,
you think you are a poet you toss me on the ground!"
the word smiled and left
left me   in writer's block.

Poem

I don't use big words
just simple deepest passion of thought
I don't don the clothes of better than
or the way of lift and slam
just sorrow from old love
gone and torn away
I don't plan on writing a poem
that would make   sense or feel
just a piece of myself
from that quilt

Thoughts

tomorrow starts a new day
tonight
is always
tonight

Poof

the blue days of night
those ones of cool
memories of hot
thoughts of   gone
new day has a few pebbles of hope
... scrambling between my words
I whisper...
hello

Evil's Playground

dark you say   you want to play
silent screams heard only in the echo
of your mind
cold stark playground alone
surrounded   alone
every moment of your inhale is pain
cascading like a million cuts into your flesh
blood follows then dries
never to end   never to end

Alone Again

blissfully dying inside
time is killing me as of late
the sun covers my slow
the breeze tells me stories of love
the ocean slams her ache across me
as I walk her edges...
but where are you
walk with me
let's make love into forever

Gone to Create

back to the basics
of life without
back to writing those books
people don't talk about
back to time with love in my soul
alone is ok ... I can do it with skill
back to...
playing pool... finding cool rocks
playing the harmonica
back to me
"gone to create"

Oh hell Again?

should have fallen that day
into the seam of life
where no love lives
no heart to keep
my beat of breath
should have opened my soul
for you to have ...
and   have
alone on my shelf of self
like a weed in the sea
floating into forever
without you... with me

Mitch Bensel

Light of Sun

starting to doubt the whispers
from the light of sun
from the way of the oceans walk
doubt is boring   but very strong
in its attempt to destroy
hope

Thoughts for a Moment

inhale my thoughts... for a moment
see if they have the taste of your soul
Thoughts for a Moment

Mitch Bensel

Gone is Me

all out of … cuddles
thrown out the hugs
kisses are drops from the stars
never finding my heart
… gone away into the woods
to listen to the trees
shift against my loss
of you … with me

Forever Blanket

ripped the wallpaper off of my memories
destroyed the table that held . . time
my pen dripped blobs of nothing
tore the cotton t-shirt off of my body
the floor gathered all
my reflection
naked
time looked at me
with forever as the blanket
I cried #life

Leftover Me

the things I find beside my thoughts
the shells of emotions I tossed
some ripped soul over there
a piece of my heart on the chair
walking away   turning on the fan
lift the old away
with a breeze of new to stay
lights off
thoughts slow
but the leftover pieces of me
flow

Dreams Wait for My Wish

I have the right whispers
and walk with shadows with easy deflection
... my kiss dissolves pain
my touch erases time...
will you open your day
for my smile...
I promise you are safe
for I am forever ...
and dreams wait form my wish

Universe

inside where time forgot
breathes me
dashed against myself
I see the beautiful of the tree
its flowers of bloom and leaves
green of tune
keep me within the within
washing self with strength
of light
bound into forever's flight
I give myself to the all
of all

No Death Today

Stop wanting to go away
never slow your life this day
to die is truly not death
so ponder the why's the if's and the
what…
be yourself live this day time and away
for the next way
your you
will find a new light

Mitch Bensel

Gone Again

he walked into the way of fog
knowing it would breathe in his soul
he let
it
for the light was over there
and he was told no
the fog   will be gentle
even though silence
would torment his heart
ever more

Ocean's Kiss

walked the beach
felt the sting of sand from the wind
that picked up everything it touched
leaned into its force
letting it clean my soul
blasting through me
taking out any old pain...
...   calm came as the salt of the ocean
settled on my skin
my ocean ...kissed me

Mitch Bensel

Sliced Time

I may have to slice time in half and jump on it like a skateboard ...
places to go   people to see ...

Poets

poets tend to know things
that the air tells only the bugs
is pretty profound place to be
... yep

Mitch Bensel

Gypsy of Life

I am a gypsy of life ...
dropping hope into hearts ...
saying hello to souls
... leaving them to live. back on my boat
... through my joy of life....
play the fiddle now
... leave with music always

Time

I may have to walk away into the image of time
it teases me with whispers to let go

Miles

miles of time lay before me
help my mind not to dive
into that pool of loss…

A Moment of Non

the scribbles of slime
the tickle of time
said to me to fall
... I hated to rhyme
so I walked in the rain
kicked a puddle
with disdain
smiled
as I fell against the wall

Mitch Bensel

A Day

into the day we go
or night if that is the way you flow
through the rooms …
coffee then food
a car may have some good old tunes
while we drive to a box
do the things
money ya know
we need it so we can
drink tequila
wear cotton t-shirts
and   dance

A Thought

between a thought ...within a breath
beside my path a place to rest
inside my heart a secret   found
I saw it ... a small of it   a piece of it
last night
was familiar yet distant covered
with maybe
and possibly or more
will ponder its hello
to see if it vanishes
or holds

Mitch Bensel

A Word

what if I was a word
pulled from your mind
through your soul
dripped into time
into your mind
circling again
and again
would I still be the word
you saw
or become what you see

Narrator

when I lean into the microphone
my breath captured and tamed
releasing rises and falls of tone
to slip across to you
vibrations are energy and life is that
so when I record a word
not only do you hear the speak
you feel it to your core
now drop your day and lean
this
way

Mitch Bensel

Surface

woke from deep
a place   never seen
ripped back against my now
I wish to be back where I was
the ripples of dreams carry out souls
like a pebble across and then sinking
depth   ... found sometimes difficult to leave
but the surface found me

WORD

I write as if I have had something to drink
hmm where was I when I slept just a bit ago
what well did I dip
my quill deeply into
the ink is black and rich with fragrance
cannot inhale it deeply enough
becoming the walk of word

Mitch Bensel

No More

follow I was the porn channel
you turned to when bored
the side desire of flavored
used
channel has been shut down

Dreams

crystalized dreams
crushed paths in my soul
opened my palm   reached
felt
gave
... glass breaks
tears liquid like rain soaking
feeding   giving
silence
hold me
echoes
know me

Contrast

when words become non
when time lies with the sun
when tomorrow cannot even speak
the darkness is winning
but cannot live   ... without contrast
then words become alive
then time flies with the sun
tomorrow screams with joy

Souls Wall

Sitting in my soul where paintings of my life move along the walls ....I saw one of those walls was empty ... sat back in time ... happy to know ... I was not quite finished

Mitch Bensel

Poetry Seen

... know the tune
take off the shoes of normal
easily find that corner hidden
oh it could be your kiss
or your boots.... that took the wrong step
poets know the dance
the lift
sometimes easy to read
other times you have to have a pass
to see the secrets

Ocean

my ocean calls me...
to soothe my soul and caress
my dreams
so much beauty in life
contrasting with ugly
ugly vanishes
in the light
choose light ... drop the britches of pain
down to the puddle of non
the air waits for your inhale
waters wait for your touch
open to beauty

A Good Day

dance a bit with your thoughts
let them tell you of peace soon to be
... hold a bit your heart
let it whisper a calm ...
today will be a good day

Positive

Never give up, we all slip down the wall and sit in the hall of pain but, we all stand back up and change our socks to slip across time

Mitch Bensel

Spider Web

Some days are like walking through a spider web, you keep feeling
the web all day and wait to feel the spider crawl across you

Near Forever

Let me have the leaf
just to rest upon
the one on the end of the branch
that is near forever
let me know peace
to rest inside
the way the sun ... calms
let me . . . be filled
with euphoria but for a moment
dripped in tired
let me rest

Mitch Bensel

Ambulance

I hear the sirens
someone is hurt
I cut their clothes
pushed on their chest
dragged their dead body
to the morgue
sirens yell
with redundancy into futility
fragile flesh matches
defeated souls ... that cry
when sirens
call

Depression

scooted my thoughts over to the window
snow covered the grounds
trees leaned with the weight
freshly covered
holding   held ...
sounds muffled
stood my thoughts in a corner
darkness there unable to move
to see the bright of fresh

Mitch Bensel

Dream

Going to whisper to my thoughts
nudge a dream to life
slowly ... inhale

Calm

I will remain calm.
I am a warrior
of love   with love   for love
peace within is peace with   out
go said myself ... go
write rambles and smash
your universe with
peace

Mitch Bensel

Notebook

scribbled messages on old school paper
crumpled notes that held a thought
the sun ran with me as a child
I carried her books
home from school....
saved her from the train
untied the ropes...
jumbled memories
notebook torn
... time

False

clothes are always the same
clean
crisp
pressed
initial hello drops all shields
the end is always the same
how many more pieces of me
can get lost in the mazes
inside false
hello

Mitch Bensel

Future Hello to Love

washing with new thoughts
flames clearing passions road
skin memories of touch
banished into forever
claiming freedom
the ocean knows my rhythm
the sands know my beat
who will know my heart
and kiss me so so
sweet

I slip

dipping my toes into the waters
fall against a splinter or two
heat holds
like it does
that liquid way of arousing
complete where only
slight moan or movement
entices the push
complete into the water
I   slip

Mitch Bensel

Energy

leftover energy
lingering against my desire
taunting me a wee bit
seeing if I will lean into
once more
once more

Underbelly

is a truth
I say to you
after your heart is broken
shattered
the tender under belly
of your soul exposed
denial of ever to seek tickles with thought
ah but the first hello
sears to the depth
and you walk once more
against their breath of now
with wishes and ease to please

Mitch Bensel

Soul Echo

words spoken
in the mind
no voice
no rhyme
gone and miss and gone again
how can a line be made
no pen to be see
no voice to hear
soul's echo
echo   ...echo

Platform of Different

we are different in ways of walk and talk
we are different in emotions
we are different in our soul's heat
we are different in our anger
in our pain
in our love
in our same
step onto the platform
stand tall
be self
be different

Mitch Bensel

Ponder

have to ponder
to walk into myself and look at
the furniture
maybe a new fireplace
or some pillows
to be comfy
to   ... make love
to find new to ease into
time

'Ting

my poet-ting broke this morning
it's a thing this -ting-
wakes all the words
scoots all the pain in one corner
arranges passion next to lust ...
with that dash of   omg...
... wait, did I just
almost looks like a poem...
-ting laughs...

Mitch Bensel

Sheers

something about the way
... the sheers of the curtains
and the breeze play

!

Lightning

lightning is the rip
of someone's soul as another leaves them
thunder is the rage of pain as the tear
digs its claws into the fabric of your essence

...

mayhaps that is why we like to make love
during thunderstorms... re birth

I Rested

my soul lay bare against the cool breeze
... your essence
I felt ... surrounded by your beauty of
time   of smile of ease
I rested

Tape

taped back together
dropped from the heights of
fantasy
I begin again

A Poem

a poem is a thought

a feel

a   sentence without

with

can be of dust the fell off into

a heart

or triumph

of a simple step

read not me with eyes of plain

the poem ...whispered

Drop

had a passion drop...
is that moment of pure
just a morsel ... just a taste
... I think I am cured

Mitch Bensel

Boiling

something is amiss
and it is in the silence
why does silence hold so much
should be vacant ...but vacant holds
emptiness   ... and empty
should be ... empty
but it is boiling over with
pain ...

Did You

did you love her...
or the idea of loving
her
is what you loved

Mitch Bensel

Crashed

crashed inside myself
silent was the way of time
but she didn't hear

Invisible

invisible thoughts deceive
with contrasting laughter
depth is shallow with a smile
silence never quiets

Darkest World

walked in the darkest world
terror was easy to feel
fed the beast of I am nothing
slipped on a shield of pity
stood to say, stood to do
stood to escape that boring brew
of pain and fear and nothing to say
... light is pulling me closer
to love of pure with ease

Star

if I looked into a star
would I see your soul
so bright upon my heart
so soft upon my lips

Mitch Bensel

Precarious

dancing with a precarious thought is just as dangerous as falling into
the pit

Whispers

Whispers never lie ... takes too much energy ... they would be silence ... I whisper ... hello sweetest one ... I watch it float across time ... cannot see if it settles but know it is from my heart

TODAY

a whisper visited me today
was from a place of soul
I know this because it took my
breath away
now   ... sometimes dots are filled
in with make believe and maybe kind of
I shall trace this whisper with my heart
and see if it   is true

Used Flavors

smell the noise of confusion
my soul spins with
used flavors
filtering through the small
crevice of shallow
thoughts ....
see me here
the small speck of used up
life
gazing at a star of empty
wishes

Slip Away

we dream of tomorrow
think of yesterday
while the moment of now
seems to just   slip away

Simply Exist

to simply exist once more enters
i thought i left this place
i feel the scraping of my fingers
down the sides of my soul as i fall
into that place of silence…

Mitch Bensel

My Air

once more i see those mirrors
the walls. the ones i watched with clothes
off   with eyes closed
my hands play with the light
eyes bored with the sight of brick
laid so perfectly... so   perfectly
i can kick the cracks and it's ok
the walls stay the same my air is the

game

Core of Humanity

Deep inside the core of humanity
is the anguish of death
its cries like thunder
thrusting into the virgin
air

Know Me

I slipped into a wave of self
tripped over shoes of old
fell through my heart
into darkness
the echo tasted like
tomorrow
the air smelled
of   love
the black fell
to the side   of hope
a journey to see
feel and know
me

Simple Way

simple way
life can be
with quality   of experience
walk the beach   feel the breeze
see the sunset   feel the sunrise
... not much left but
simple way
for me

Mitch Bensel

Avalanche

the avalanche of life
hit me today
within the caverns of
complication and
responsibility
saddened
but hopeful

Woke Up

was walking in the clouds
they were full of wishes and dreams
like flowers across an open field
... daisies I think
some looked down then fell away
like the rain
onto people walking   ...
wishes find us
dreams are real
I tripped over tomorrow
and woke up

Mitch Bensel

Subtle Thoughts

subtle thoughts are dangerous
they move without thinking
ponder that

Inside Myself

kind of lost inside myself
walked beside myself...
no u turns everywhere
sat for a bit in the rain ...
or did i cry
wait that was a movie not I

Mitch Bensel

Memory of You

Slicing through the way of my day
... walking with a dot of strength
I slipped against a memory
... with only your smile to blame

No Banter

I don't banter with darkness
or let it visit my porch
there are no chairs for it to sit upon
and I offer it no smokes
it walks on by...
never even tries...
not welcome near the light of love
or to toss its anger at me
done with that never again
for my eyes to see

Mitch Bensel

The Trees Play

I watched the trees today
the wind moved them
they were playing tag   reaching
could almost hear their laughter
... as the leaves danced along
the air ...I feel also enjoyed the exchange

Darkness Play

dark you say you want to play
silent screams heard only in the echo
of your mind
cold stark playground alone
surrounded   alone
every moment of your inhale is pain
cascading like a million cuts into your flesh
blood follows then dries
never to end ... never to end

Mitch Bensel

Time's Kiss

a kiss upon a soul ...
breath into a heart
anguish comes sealed with pain
... tomorrow never sings
... rain doesn't fall
dry is time's kiss
on my wish

Walls of Self

restless inside my walls of self
waiting for passion to whisper good morning
not sure I can wait
have to walk the streets naked
my soul exposed to chill the passion
she creates…
… don't need training wheels
but some shoes might help

Beauty of Self

flowers are not shy
they show all their beauty
for the sun to explore   touch …
they lean into the sunset whispering
resting in the night
breathe in their truth... open your soul
rest in the calm beauty   ... of yourself

Demons and Dust Balls

Demons they are real like dust balls and alligators
doesn't mean they can bother ya ...
walk around the gators sweep up the dust balls ...

End

fell into a tear

or was it a lake   deeper than air

falling I became a leaf

abandoned by my tree

killing me ... it dropped

me

... the air told me stories

... drifted into

my end

About the Author

Mitch Bensel is an International, multi genre author and narrator. A parent of three daughters and a grandparent to two grandsons. He loves the ocean with its amazing energies and treasures, agates and jaspers. Look for his books on Amazon, Barnes & Noble, iTunes, and many places on the net.
Thank you for reading — Twitter Poetry ~ Love and Life — Visit his you tube Mitch Bensel, and enjoy wonderful narrations of phenomenal writings from author's around the world and his poetry.

Made in the USA
Middletown, DE
02 August 2022

70326782R00186